JEAN LORRAIN

THE TURKISH LADY
AND OTHER WRITINGS

THIS IS A SNUGGLY BOOK

ISBN: 978-1-64525-136-1

The contents of the current volume are significantly revised versions of translations which previously appeared in various places.

"Jean Lorrain" (1855-1906) was the pseudonym of Paul Duval, adopted at the insistence of his father, a Norman ship-owner, who wanted to protect the family name from the disgrace of employment by a poet. A flamboyant homosexual dandy, when forced to make a living from his pen after his father died ruined, he became one of the most prolific and highest-paid journalists of the *fin-de-siècle*, and the personification, in his lifestyle as well as his writing, of the Decadent Movement. *Monsieur de Phocas. Astarté* (1901; tr. as *Monsieur de Phocas*), compounded out of numerous short stories, is a kind of retrospective summary of the Decadent world-view, written after he was forced to leave Paris because of health problems occasioned by his use of ether as a stimulant, which did not take long to kill him thereafter. English translations of some of his short stories are contained in *Nightmares of an Ether-Drinker* (Snuggly Books, 2016), *The Soul-Drinker and Other Decadent Fantasies* (Snuggly Books, 2016) and *Masks in the Tapestry* (Snuggly Books, 2017).

CONTENTS

THE TURKISH LADY
AND OTHER WRITINGS

THE TURKISH LADY

THE young Turkish woman on board the *Asia*, which carried us from Tripoli to Malta, was the charm, the poem and the enigma of the voyage.

The *Asia!* How many pictures that name brings up before my mind.

I see myself once again leaning against the railing, on a radiant Sunday morning, and feel again the same sensations which came to me as I looked upon her sweet face.

Tripoli appeared in all its beauty to wish us a last farewell.

White and shining on the sea, it was the city of mirages, the Turkish city of which we had dreamed so much, with its green towers and domes clearly outlined against the transparent azure sky. And there the palace of the Pasha, the Mule, the silhouettes of the walls and the little boats of the sponge fishers, lying about the quay in the shade of the ramparts.

Then before me appeared the incarnation of this Islam we were about to leave. She was exotic by her costume and enigmatic by her beauty. Her walk was Oriental, slow and graceful; she was Oriental from her eyes, blackened with charcoal, to her hair, bleached with huma leaves.

Enveloped from head to foot in a black satin mantle, I took her for a Maltese, for she had taken off her veil, and in the distance I thought her cloak a faldetta; but a woman from Malta would not have smoked a cigarette, and with what charm and indolence of gesture this one smoked hers.

Evidently she was an experienced smoker, and the points of her slightly yellow-tinted fingers revealed the Oriental initiated, from childhood, in kief and narghila.

She was sitting upon a bench and speaking with an officer of the Sultan, who, with other officers, had conducted her on board.

He, too, was smoking, and when I expressed surprise at this—the man smoking before sundown and the woman revealing the mystery of her face—I was answered that the believer was absolved from all restraint, and fasting, as soon as he left the Holy Land. "Holy Land" is Turkish for all followers of Allah: the sea belongs to no one, and the obligation of the Mahomedan who travels is only to say five prayers, morning, noon and night.

So, approaching the group, I blessed this laxity of the usually severe laws of the Koran, for the passenger of the *Asia* revealed to my eyes one of the most delicious faces that I had ever seen.

The chin was slightly square, the lips strongly cut, the mouth sinuous and as fresh as a pomegranate, opening over grains of enamel—a Turkish mouth which seemed made for kisses—and large blue-gray eyes embedded in long dark lashes.

The face was tormented and sad, with something tragical and voluptuous about it. I was immediately drawn toward her. And when she smiled, it was with the abandon of the most provoking coquette.

The *Asia* glided over the smooth sea and the Turkish woman continued to smoke with the officer, under the respectful but incomprehensible eyes of her suite—a negro and two negresses—enveloped in silk and veils.

Through discretion, I retired to one side and amused myself by examining the luggage of the stranger—bundles of colored stuff and a sumptuous box of copper.

This honey-combed, reddish-brown box could tell a long tale about this lady's home.

"A Pasha's wife," someone whispered in my ear. "Her husband is exiled. She went to Tripoli to obtain an escort and permission to go and find him in the sands, for he is in the desert, at Fezzan. But the Pasha of Tripoli would not give her the escort, and she is returning to Beirut by way of Alexandria. We go to take a boat at

Malta. I am the interpreter, and am traveling with her."

"And you, a Jew?" I said, quickly.

"One says not Jew, but Israelite," replied he, and the voice of the man seemed to caress and ask pardon. "Say Israelite; you do not love Jews. I am Armenian."

"Why should I have anything against you, when I see you for the first time? Your mistress is Mussulman?"

"Yes, and she is pretty, my mistress. Eh! She pleases you?"

"She pleases me vastly more than you, certainly; here is for your complaisance," and I slipped two francs into his hand. "Goodbye; have you been long in her service?"

"Since this morning. She paid my passage for acting as interpreter. Me speak the English, the French a little, and very well the Turkish and Italian. At your service, Master. Me be happy to do something for you. Me likes you already."

"Really! Take these cigarettes. Goodbye until tomorrow."

I turned around. The Turkish lady had disappeared.

The *Asia* began to roll; the sea, which had been so calm on leaving the Syote, was now growing restless. The deck was soon deserted.

The wife of the Pasha was probably ill, but where? In the second-class cabin, without doubt, because my mother and myself were the only first-class passengers. This Pasha's wife perplexed me: this long voyage, undertaken far from the harem, to find an adored husband, or, who knows? a hated tyrant. Her failure at Tripoli, her many useless efforts and vicissitudes, the tragedy of the soul and perhaps of the palace which this exiled widow carried with her, the mystery of her adventure, joined to the charm of her mysterious beauty—all this excited me and filled me with the most tormenting thoughts.

In the morning I went upon the foam-covered deck; only the officers on watch were to be seen. I did not see her until the next day, and then I saw her in confusion and in the complete abandonment of all coquetry. Through a large opening on the part of the ship reserved for third-class passengers she tossed upon a mattress, inert, and racked with suffering.

Her two women knelt beside her in the attitude of animals, while her man-servant watched in a corner.

How distressing it was to see this young woman of a different race and religion, thrown by hazard upon this European vessel, with no other protection than these three black slaves, and with only the loyalty of an unknown and equivocal interpreter to depend upon.

I contemplated her for a long time. She was still charming in her disorder and paleness, charming in spite of the ravages sea-sickness had made upon her beauty.

The satin hood with which her head was enveloped the previous evening had fallen off her shoulders, and her pretty head appeared amidst the falling waves of her hair.

The Turkish officer was not beside her; this, at least, was a solace for me. I should have suffered had he been there.

At this moment she lifted her eyes and blushed, ashamed of her flowing hair. She tried to draw her hood over her head, but was too weak, and, half raising herself upon her elbow, she whispered something to her women. With a bound the negresses were upon their feet, and in the twinkling of an eye a drapery screened her face from view.

Then they built an Asiatic wall before my eyes. In a few moments they had constructed a tent of red and yellow cotton, but uneasiness agitated them still behind their pavilion, for all the folds of the tent oscillated from the contact of black fingers, and in this improvised retreat was to be heard an indigenous chatter and angry exclamations in the Turkish language.

My presence disturbed them. I became discreet, but a little too late. I went to the fore part of the vessel, and, in spite of the tossing, which was worse here, I became absorbed in the contemplation of Malta: Malta, this mass of rocks, visited since sunrise, and yet seemingly as far off as ever.

※

Oh! this passage of the Maltese channel; it is the worst part of the Mediterranean. This boisterous sea, with the short, heavy waves surging against the vertically cut rocks; these invisible rocks, whose neighborhood one feels in the sudden violence of the waves, and this irritating and deceiving island of dreams called Malta.

Malta, with its high line of mountains and cliffs standing straight like a wall above the waves crested with foam.

Malta, the rampart of Christianity against the Oriental world.

Malta, the Island of Chevaliers.

It was the Island of Chimeras and Mirages on this January morning, under this wan-looking sky, where the mountains seemed to diminish instead of becoming larger, a fugitive island, which seemed to recede in the fog as the *Asia* advanced.

※

Then, at last, La Valette detaches itself from the stony mass of the island—La Valette, with its palaces, houses, churches and streets in the form of an amphitheatre. It seems as if the high towers were sculptured in old ivory. The terraces and palaces seem to mount as high as the sky or descend into the sea.

La Valette is built entirely of Maltese marble. It reminds one of an immense hospital for lepers, as one looks at the ruined silhouette of this city without trees, without verdure, and so isolated in its enclosure of waves which beat upon it so mercilessly.

Malta is of a yellow color, yellow as gold even under its gray sky. Its stone, of an ivory color, seems to retain the reverberation of the sun, and this golden transparence—which bathes in winter, as well as in summer, certain portions of Marseilles, this halo of savage clearness, which astonishes and distresses the Northerner like a breath of the plague—is the glory of Malta and the pride of the Maltese.

Finally, we were at anchor, and then the Turkish woman appeared, wearing her silk haik, and with only her eyes visible—her large eyes with the heavy lids, whereon weariness had left its stamp.

She was leaning upon the arm of the Turkish officer, and I felt a painful sensation at my heart.

Her servants followed her, and the Armenian interpreter said:

"Shiamé Esmirli, wife of Essad-Bey, twenty-eight years, going to Haggi, near Beirut, from Turkey in Asia, she and her followers."

The interpreter gave a list of Turkish names, then told his own: "Bascia Cahuaji, born at Alexandria, of Armenian parentage."

Shiamé Esmirli was her name, sonorous and soft as the song of a bird!

At a word from the interpreter, she detached her haik and submitted to the examination of the physician, which all the passengers had to undergo before being permitted to land. How pale and languishing she looks today, and still more mysterious, since I have learned her name: Shiamé Esmirli. Where is she going to stay in Malta?

I was so troubled that I did not even hear. "Hotel Constantinople," whispered the Armenian, Bascia Cahuaji, in my ear, and be stretched out his hand at the same time for a tip.

That Armenian! I should like to beat him. But porters were now taking possession of our luggage.

A bark was bringing Shiamé Esmirli to shore; she was seated beside the Sultan's officer.

Hotel Constantinople! What pretext can I make for speaking to her? I thought she smiled at me when she was taking off her haik.

At ten o'clock, on the morning of the third day, it was raining like a deluge, when a visitor was announced. Since our arrival there had been nothing but showers and squalls. One would say that a cyclone of water raged on the "Island of Chevaliers."

"Jean, a visitor," my mother's voice called from her room. These rooms of the Australian Hotel were high as cathedrals and inlaid with marble like a palace, and yet, notwithstanding that these walls were plastered with delf, they were swarming with insects.

A visitor! It must be the consul? I finished arranging my tie and then went, by the exterior gallery, with its stone columns, to the next room.

Entering, I could scarcely refrain from crying out. There was a deputation of negroes and people from the Orient in their native dress, with turbans of bright silk, and in the midst of them was the Turkish lady who had traveled with us from Tripoli.

She arose from her chair, and, with exquisite grace, made two steps towards me, slightly inclining herself, and, with lowered eyes, saluted me *à la Turque*, that is to say, she placed her hand to her forehead, then to her heart, and finally to her lips, then slowly kissing the back of her hand she remained in this inclined attitude for a moment and made the last gesture, which seemed to waft the kiss towards me.

Ah! this pretty Turkish greeting of such eloquent mimic, where in these three gestures the Oriental offers you everything—for you my head, for you my heart, for you my lips.

For me her thoughts, for me her heart, for me her mouth—her mouth in this kiss on the back of her hand. I was stunned.

Shiamé Esmirli, the wife of the Pasha of Beirut, has called upon me! I cannot understand it.

She seated herself again and waited for Bascia Cahuaji to explain why she had come.

Bascia Cahuaji, the Jewish interpreter! I might have guessed, in fact, that only he could have brought her here. I began to hate his caressing eyes and the irritating gesture of his hands. The volubility of Bascia exerted itself to explain to us that Shiamé Esmirli, touched by our solicitude, wished to thank us for the interest we had taken in her.

The interest which we had taken in her! My mother did not understand, but I did.

The previous evening, while loitering in the Street Santa Ursola, I had noticed, written above a large gate, Hotel Constantinople.

I remembered that the Turkish woman was to stop there, and, uneasy at not having seen her for three days at the quarantine, I entered and inquired for her of the porter. Quarantine? Yes, I have forgotten to mention an unpleasant task we were obliged to perform during our stay in Malta. Every morning, from nine until ten, we had to present ourselves, with the Levantin and Italian sailors from Africa, before the spectacles of the English doctors.

The negroes and the Armenian Jew were always there, but Shiamé Esmirli did not appear. My curiosity, my unreasonable desire to inquire after her at her inn, was the cause of this visit of gratitude from the beautiful Shiamé, but how had this Armenian ruffian discovered our address?

"His mistress was deeply grateful for our inquiries; she had noticed us during the voyage, and was glad that an opportunity to make our acquaintance had presented itself. She was so lonely, in Malta, where she was obliged to remain still two days in awaiting the boat for Alexandria. She was alone in this English city. The Turkish officer had returned to Constantinople. She was at the verge of despair in this unknown city, under this beating rain, and it was a source of great joy to her when she learned that someone in Malta took an interest in her.

"She had been very ill, but my advances had nearly cured her, and she wished to come and present her respects to my mother and thank me. We were, no doubt, Parisians. Ah! Paris! It was her dread to go there. She would be willing never again to see Beirut if we would take them to Paris. Shiamé offered us her slaves; they were her property and worth five thousand francs: the women fifteen hundred francs each, and the man two thousand; we could have them at once even if we did not wish to take Shiamé to Paris. She did not care to send them back to Asia; the voyage was so expensive, and they would certainly feel happier with us than with her. Her poor old servants were so devoted to her, and only bad treatment awaited them upon their return to Asia, for what pity could the slaves of a mistress in disgrace expect?

"Shiamé had been very unfortunate: she was the second wife of the Pasha of Beirut, but was the most beloved. She had no children, while the first wife had two sons. The husband of Shiamé was sixty, and she was eighteen when she married. As long as he resided in Beirut Shiamé had lived in peace, for the other wife was afraid of the Pasha and dared not attempt anything against Shiamé. But since he had displeased the Sultan in. the affairs relating to Armenia, the Sultan had exiled him to Fezzan, and the other wife had assumed full authority in the house. It was thus that Shiamé, through humiliation, had undertaken this journey. She had obtained a passport from the Turkish authorities and had deserted the harem, carrying her silver and jewels with her. Her husband was one of the first generals of the Porte, but he was a Liberal, had lived a long time in Paris, and after the massacres of Armenia had signed the list of protestation of the Turkish students, for even Turks had protested against the ignominies and exactions of the Janizary.

"Essad Bey was stripped of all power, and, what was still worse, exiled to Fezzan in disgrace.

"Fezzan is among the sands, hundreds of miles away from Tripoli.

"It is there that Shiamé wished to rejoin her husband, but one could not venture there without an escort. It is the most dangerous part of East Africa. But the escort had been refused her by Mehri-Ahmet Bey, and the young woman, sad and discouraged, was obliged to return from whence she came. She might as well be exiled, for what welcome could she expect upon her return?

"Would she even be received by the other wife, who was the mother of the sons of Essad? The sons of the Pasha could repudiate her, in the name of their father, for revolting and fleeing.

"And all this was the cause of the sorrow of Shiamé Esmirli.

"If she could only interest someone in her behalf—for example, ourselves—how easily she would renounce her title of favorite and consent never again to return to the East."

And with smiles of pity, with eyes raised heavenwards and supplications of entreaty, it was with expressive mimic and passionate gesticulation that Bascia Cahuaji underlined his story, while Shiamé Esmirli continued to smile, ashamed, I think, of her role of beautiful mute and so many words which she could not comprehend.

I ordered Turkish coffee (politeness exacts this throughout Islam) and Shiamé sipped it slowly, her beautiful gray eyes looking into mine; she could not dream what strange thoughts for her were passing within me.

Was there any truth in all this? Was she, in reality, the heroine of this Armenian story— Shiamé Esmirli transfigured by love, rejected love, and a wandering victim of conjugal duty; or did not this beauty, perilous to those who watched her, this liberty of manners, this charm and apparent unconsciousness of the daring of her conduct, rather disclose a dreaded adventuress?

Before her profoundly innocent eyes, tranquilly looking into mine, I desired to believe in the veracity of the interpreter's story; yet when I looked at the Armenian, the equivocal companion was so enveloped in a heavy atmosphere of baseness that I could not reconcile the idea of a general's wife coming and hunting up strangers in their hotel, accompanied by this ruffian.

He sipped his coffee and watched me with a strange look which made me nervous and filled me with resentment.

The three servants took their coffee standing, posed like statues; outside the rain had redoubled its violence and fell in torrents upon the exterior gallery.

Malta in a shower, Malta in a squall, a whole island under water. At last our Turkish visitor arose to take her leave: she pressed our hands with effusion, and prayed us to allow her to come again; "we were the only friends she had in Malta." Cahuaji translated this for us.

I conducted her to the door. We were upon the threshold. "Come tonight to the Café de la Rotonde," whispered the Armenian in my ear. "Come about nine o'clock. Shiamé Esmirli wishes to speak to you alone."

Tonight at the Café de la Rotonde!

I did not go. That same evening our luggage was being transported from the Australian Hotel to the Imperial; we had been chased by invisible insects from the palatial Australian Hotel.

I had only to cross the street to find Shiamé Esmirli, but why did she wish for a private interview with me? Wife of the Pasha! what an invention! So, throwing myself, all dressed, upon my bed, I passed the evening in excusing myself for my want of gallantry in refusing to comply with her request. In fact, a sort of unconscious perversity kept me in my room and made me delight in not appearing at the trysting-place. I was angry with myself for being suspicious of her, but this obsequious and crooked Armenian Jew was to blame. Afterward he pursued me at the hotel and forced an entrance to my room, saying that I had caused his mistress much sorrow, that Shiamé Esmirli felt very kindly towards me, that she ardently desired to see me. He insisted that I should make another appointment to see her for that evening at the same place, because, on account of her slaves, Shiamé Esmirli could not receive me in her hotel.

This time I kept my word, but at the café I found only Bascia Cahuaji. The Armenian had come alone; his mistress, feeling ill, was unable to accompany him, but if I would be good enough to follow him, we would go to her. The scruples which prevented her seeing me at her hotel had doubtless melted away. The poor Shiamé was very homesick; it was a good deed to pay her a visit. "You not have your rings today? You have for much money worth of rings?"

I did not like this question. What mattered it to him if I wore my rings or not?

I declined his offer to go to Shiamé, and it seemed to me that he insisted less than usual; one would imagine that my forgotten rings had cooled his ardor. We parted, I promising to see her in the morning, at the same place. I found the Turkish lady there with her man-servant, the negresses having remained at the hotel. I was late—gallant again. Shiamé arose, and, raising her hand to her forehead, to her heart, and then to her lips, repeated her pretty Turkish salute. It seemed to me as if she had been weeping: her heavy eyelids were red; she seemed pale, but upon looking more closely,

I saw that it was the effect of *poudre de riz*;
her lips were painted and her hands were very
much perfumed. She offered them to me for
the first time. Was it conceitedness on my part?
I thought she pressed my fingers.

Cahuaji told me that I had done well to
come, and that his mistress was very happy.
Shiamé showed her white, shining teeth, and
remained immobile. Cahuaji took my hand;
he whispered to his mistress, calling attention
to my hands. She stooped to admire them and
to take my hand in hers.

"She thinks your rings very beautiful; the
blue stone pleases her much; she says it resem-
bles your eyes; what is the name of the stone?"

"Sapphire."

"Sapphire, how pretty! My mistress has also
rings, but she wears only one today." And the
officious Cahuaji placed the hand of Shiamé
within mine.

She wore an opal upon the annular finger,
a troubled milky opal almost without reflec-
tion, an oblong stone with blue veins, vulgar-
ly set in a large silver ring. Out of politeness
I admired it.

"It belongs to you, if you desire it; my mistress gives it, as well as her slaves, to you. It is a wedding present from the Pasha. Do you not want the ring? She would be pleased for you to wear her ring." The Turkish lady smiled with her beautiful, sinuous mouth. "Why not exchange rings, you two? You give the sapphire, my mistress the opal."

"This sapphire was given to me."

And upon this I arose; I made a pretext for returning home. "You not pleased; me displease you; you excuse me."

Shiamé, impassible and silent, continued to smile; a humid light entered her eyes; a perfume of amber and jasmine surrounded her. I loved and hated her!

"Is she an accomplice of this ruffian, or is she only a blind plaything in his hands? Is she ignorant, or does she know?"

My rudeness made me ashamed, and I asked permission to conduct her to her hotel.

She took my arm; it seemed to me that in the obscure little streets she leaned upon me rather more than was necessary, but then, this

Armenian had put ignominious ideas into my head. At last he was quiet, and this silent *tête-à-tête* with this beautiful woman on my arm in the labyrinth of solitary streets was delicious.

The next day Cahuaji came to say farewell. They were leaving at noon on that day, but Shiamé was in great trouble.

When she brought him, Cahuaji, from Tripoli, she had not counted the cost; her passage back was paid, but his was not; herefore she was obliged to leave him in Malta because she had not the money to pay for him. She was two hundred francs short, and that was the reason of her sorrow. She had no one in whom she could confide, although he had assured her that she could tell me her trouble, as he had noticed my admiration yesterday. Would I accept the opal and pay two hundred francs? It was worth twice that sum, but for ten louis I could accept a remembrance from his mistress and thus deliver them from a source of great anxiety.

And the ruffian drew the opal from within his handkerchief. I was duped. It pleased me to think that Shiamé was ignorant of all this. I gave the desired sum. The man kissed my hands, and, had I allowed it, would have kissed my feet.

"You will come on board to wish her farewell?"

"Yes, if I can. Adieu!"

He was gone and I had her opal on my finger, the opal of Shiamé Esmirli; she was leaving and I should not see her again—Shiamé Esmirli, the wife of the Pasha, or Esmirli the adventuress?

The Armenian had told me falsehoods, falsehoods and falsehoods again!

I am twice their dupe. They have not gone. Oh, how they must have ridiculed my simplicity in their barbarous, caressing, and yet metallic language. When she met me I felt revengeful, and turned upon my heels to avoid her.

She was to have gone at noon, yet at four o'clock she wandered nonchalantly and with curiosity across the streets, accompanied by her escort of negresses and leaning upon the arm of her interpreter, an Oriental princess in the center of her suite, but a princess trained to raise money from travelers impressed by her beautiful eyes.

I was wearing her opal; mechanically I took it off and put it in my pocket.

It burned my flesh, now that I saw the little machination to which it had served. Besides, it was very ugly, and the opal is unlucky. I returned to the hotel, threw the ring into a valise and went aimlessly wandering about where the soldiers of Her Most Gracious Majesty employ their time in getting intoxicated. Here, at least, I was in safety against the temptations of Shiamé Esmirli, in safety against myself, for I could not meet her here. Whatever happened, I was quite decided not to see her again.

A logical decision, which did not prevent my saying to the coachman to return by the Hotel Constantinople. But the place seemed hermetically closed. How long would she remain at the inn? Perhaps she would leave in the morning, and then I should never see her again, she who had been my very life since the evening when she appeared upon the deck of the *Asia*, in the amber and rosy gold of this divine twilight.

Why had she postponed her departure? Perhaps she desired to see me, and I was accusing her of complicity with this Jew! She was ignorant of his baseness. I excused her; I acquitted her of all blame, and I would see her not later than the following morning; it was stupid of me to be eternally going against my desires.

But the next day I passed at Città Vecchia, the dead city, the ancient capital of Malta, situated at one hour's distance from La Valette. Città Vecchia, where the footsteps of the visitor in the middle of the streets, bordered with palaces, do not draw one face to the window. Città Vecchia, where you meet no one except three guides at the station, the porter of the Cathedral and the beadle.·

It was in this tomb, this dust of centuries, and this infinite sadness that I voluntarily put in a whole day at one hour's distance from La Valette, where I knew she was. Why?

There are days when one likes to suffer and make others suffer, hours when the quintessence of joy is to torture your own heart. I returned to La Valette late for dinner.

I was told that she had sent to inquire for me; I was furious and yet overjoyed to think she pursued me so incessantly.

She came to say goodbye in my absence. They have gone down to the port. I descend, four by four, the stairs of Santa Lucia and arrive at the gate of Dogana. In the refreshing shade of its arches Esmirli appears, such a picture in a frame of heaven's blue and the blue of the sea.

What a picture is this Port of Malta, with its shining waters, its scattered barques, its comings and goings, its clanking chains, its trucks and the gesticulations of all these thickset, sunburned Maltese people.

It is noon, all is life and gaiety; in this mirthfulness and this light I see her again, pale, smiling and sad, already stamped with the irreparable seal of those who must part. She comes to me. She does not make the three ceremonial bows; spontaneously she places her hand in mine, while she looks right into my soul. Cahuaji explains to me, with many gestures of his long, flexible hands, that Shiamé is very happy at seeing me, and that I have been very cruel to her; that she remained only to see me.

Tender reproaches, remarkable in the mouth of Cahuaji, shaded with caressing intonations, but I tolerate them, because they are underlined this time by the tearful eyes and the pressure of her hand.

We shall see each other again at the Café de la Rotonde and pass this last evening together. This time Shiamé's fingers insist upon it, and her eyes beg me to accord her this last favor; I promise.

Afterward the Armenian came to beg a photograph of me.

"Portrait of you, bring tonight to the café. Shiamé will keep it forever in remembrance of you who was good to her. You will bring it?"

And he really has the eyes of a good, faithful dog in saying this.

At the Café de la Rotonde that evening Shiamé was pale and mute. She smiled with her pretty mouth, and her large gray eyes were fastened upon me. She looked at the photograph fixedly, then at me, as if she wanted to make sure of the resemblance; but all at once she frowned, speaking to Cahuaji, who said:

"Why do you not wear the ring which she gave you? If you did not like it, you should not have accepted it."

I explain to Cahuaji that an opal brings ill-luck, that a bad influence is attributed to it.

Cahuaji repeated my words to Shiamé; she listened pensively, then arising, with a grave smile, she said to the Armenian, who, in his turn, repeated to me:

"If the opal is a stone of ill-omen in Europe, it is the symbol of devotedness in Asia; it is a sign of abnegation and love, of even unreciprocated love, a sign of slavery, the nuptial stone. That is why she has offered it to you. She had been happy to think it would give you pleasure. Shiamé is leaving tomorrow, and is very tired. She begs you not to accompany her to her hotel."

I insisted, but Shiamé was now perfectly impassible. Her hand, which I seized, remained cold and inert. I felt the uselessness of any further attempt towards undoing what I had unhappily done in wounding her by not wearing the ring.

"You leave tomorrow at noon?"

"Yes."

"Irrevocably?"

"Yes."

"Upon what boat?"

"The *Neva*."

"I shall go and wish you goodbye."

We have just returned from the *Neva*—we, for my mother wished to say goodbye to Shiamé. We found her installed upon the bridge reserved for third-class passengers, surrounded by her slaves and the Armenian. I saw again the historical trunk which had perplexed me so much, and, like the first day, I admired and sadly longed for these beautiful, placid, aquamarine eyes. These beautiful, tender eyes, like mist and like the waves, they were so mysteriously blue, green and gray; more than ever I regretted the sinuous mouth and the short, glittering teeth.

Shiamé, visibly happy at our visit, asked my mother to kiss her. Shiamé also offered me her soft, downy cheek to kiss. Shall we ever meet again?

In parting, Shiamé, leaning over the ship, watched us descending the stairs; her eyes never left us.

My mother remarked this, but what she did not see and never will know was the gesture of Shiamé when I slipped the opal ring into her hand, the opal which brings bad luck in superstitious Europe, the opal, a sign of devotion in marvelous Asia.

Shiamé tremblingly took the ring, then she opened her hand, and, with bent eyes, a faint smile on her lips, she threw this token of devotion, which I had not accepted, and of bad luck, which she now feared, into the sea.

THE LAST DAYS OF VENICE

Venice!

Ah, Venice, thou siren of sea cities, sprung from the ocean's foam, even as Venus did, with thy wealth of soft, blue skies and water, and of art and architecture, thou art indeed the fairest daughter of the Adriatic, the Venus of the world.

—English author.

AND this city of cities is in danger, is threatened with destruction, oblivion! Should the architects and engineers summoned to ward off the impending peril be unable to devise some means of staying the shifting soil and of bracing the pile-work which forms the foundations of the city, if science comes not to assistance of art endangered, then Venice, the fair bride of the Adriatic, must become a second Ys. And it will be necessary to open no dykes to bring about the submergence. Venice will entomb herself in the dark waters of her own canals.

For centuries her soil has been settling. Hour by hour the pavements of her palaces incline more and more toward the bottom of the lagoon. Pillars are sinking—the capitals of the Doges' Palace are no longer true; the rich mosaic work which once formed so beautiful a marble carpet at the Basilica of St. Marks is now cracked, broken and sadly disfigured.

Along the Grand Canal—that most unique thoroughfare of the world, bordered by beautiful palaces and sunny gardens—the ancient buildings have lost their alignment and threaten to topple over at any time, Already they have been condemned by the municipality. Their fall would jeopardize the adjoining palaces. The least attempt at repair would be a source of danger to the city itself, so unstable is the soil.

Some steps in the way of prevention and restoration were taken five or six years ago, when Casa d'Oro was rescued from destruction. Since then attention has been turned to the Labia Palace, now a cloth manufactory, the old banqueting hall of which contains, perhaps, the finest Tieopolos in the world. On the other hand, however, as though to strike a balance, the Palace of Dario, a rare gem of architecture on the Grand Canal, is shortly to be demolished, and its subversion will be accompanied by that of the Abbalia, a curious little abbey in close proximity.

Fortunately, the Palace of Dario is owned by an enthusiastic Venetian lady. She resolved to put up a duplicate of the old palace; and, to facilitate the work of reconstruction, every stone is now being numbered, and the entire facade, with all its arabesque marble adornments, will be re-erected on new foundations.

It is to be regretted that all the palaces in danger are not the property of the broad-minded Countess de Baume Pluvinel; even to-day along the Grand Canal may be seen many vacant lots. The Campanile, the old bell tower of the city, was the first to go. In 1902, with its foundations all eaten away, it collapsed in a huge cloud of dust and with a terrific noise. In its fall it destroyed the marvelous Logetta, perhaps the most curious bit of Venetian art in bronze and marble, and a corner of the Library—ten meters of the porticoes, sculptured windows and balustrades—thus disfiguring the whole of the Piazzetta and one entire side of the Plaza.

And yet, in its fall, had it but struck St. Marks or even the Palace of the Doges opposite, the Campanile would have wrought far greater havoc. The facade of St. Marks, once damaged, would be irreparable; as for the Palace of the Doges, its condition is such that nothing could have saved it. The foundations have sunk to so great an extent that experts believe it has been actually saved by the fall of the Campanile. One of the two had to go, the bell tower or the ducal palace.

Hideous scaffoldings and boardings now mark the sites of the Campanile and the Logetta. The latter may some day grace the city once more, for photographs and models permit of its reconstruction, but the Campanile never. The soil, undermined as it is, could never support the enormous weight of such a building again, although the Venetians, for fear of alarming strangers, are slow to admit this.

It has once been well said that St. Marks represents the religion and the faith of Venice. If so, the Palace of the Doges is its history, its art. In this palace there are all the glories of the republic—its battles, its victories over the Turks, the Veronese, the Pisans; its secular struggles against the Genoese. Lepanto and Don Juan of Austria, Callaro and Zara, the taking of Constantinople, Frederic Barbarossa on his knees before the gates of St. Mark's, the papal ambassadors to the Senate, coronations, intrigues, Catarina Cornaro and the contentions at the court of Chipre, Henry III at Venice, Sicily *en échec*, proclaimed, sung and painted on the ceilings and on the walls of more than eighteen rooms, by Bassano, Palma, Titian, Tintoretto, Veronese; while in the center of the Hall of the Council of Ten there flames the grand, the immortal *Venice Triumphant* of Paolo Caliari! In short, the Palace of the Doges is drama and literature combined; it is Marino Falieri on the staircase of the Giants; it is the

Venice Saved of Otway, and, before Casimir Delavigne, it is *Othello*, the *Merchant of Venice* and the finest of Shakespeare's dramas.

And even this great palace is sinking. Scaffoldings dishonor the halls. The sacred silence of years is desecrated by the noisy clatter of the artisans at work, repairing and strengthening the walls; huge canvases, the delight of generations, have been rudely displaced and are now carelessly piled upon the floors as though in the center of a studio; forgotten frescoes have come to light from behind the paintings of Bossano and Titian, now removed only to be destroyed by hammer and chisel. The sight of all these glories, of all these annals, fallen into the ruthless hands of workmen, is so depressing that a visit now to the old palace is a thing too sad to be enjoyed.

And these workmen are everywhere. Bare, hideous framework now surrounds the Procuraties—the ancient, time-honored Procuraties of Lombardo, of Barthelomeo Buone, of Bergamasco. That part of the building which overlooks the little canal and the short, narrow street in the rear is already doomed, held up as it is only by heavy timbers extending from the opposite side of the street.

There are scaffoldings in the Church of Giovanni e Paulo and in that of the Frari—the churches of the tombs and second only to St. Mark's in the magnificence of their architecture and sculpture. Rows of wooden posts support the arcades before the Quadri, the whole of St. Mark's Place is hidden by scaffolding, and even in the grand old church itself can be seen the same old, heart-rending sights of workmen and repair.

The Church of the Frari—the Pantheon of Venice—formerly contained the remains of the great generals and admirals of the Loredans, the Vandramins, the Venieres, the Valiers, the Corners. The entire Golden Book of the Venetian nobility was piled up there in the two gloomy aisles of San Giovanni—a magnificent array of tombs. The majority of the statues have now fallen from the marble sarcophagi placed on high, in niches in the walls; the winged victories of the allegories which once veiled them have followed them to the dusty gloom of the sacristies. The marks of danger and decay are everywhere. The weight of so much glory, immortalized in marble and metal, has become a source of danger to the church. Immense crevasses, plainly visible in the walls, have appeared. To repair them it is necessary that all this splendor be removed.

The same lamentable spectacle awaits one at the Church of San Giovani. Here they have removed the bodies of the Doges, just as from the Church of the Frari the bodies of the generals and admirals have been withdrawn. A row of planking conceals the mausoleum of Canova; a boarding dishonors the choir and the handsome stalls; the sacristy, with its woodwork in the style of the Renaissance, has become the prey of carpenters. At the Church of the Frari they have even pulled down the paintings of the Virgin of Bellini and the two Tiepolos in the ceilings.

Cracks and fissures are the enemies of Venice. And they are omnipresent. In the Basilica, the churches, walls have been laid open by them, foundations undermined, ceilings rent asunder.

The Venetians, if they would save Venice from becoming a second city of Ys on the Adriatic, must awaken to its dangers. As the inheritors of the richest treasures of centuries, they owe it to the world and to posterity to rescue their city from destruction. Venice must be saved!

THE PRINCESS OF THE GEESE

THE servants had removed the dishes, the venison, and the heavy honey cakes, and the pages had come to lead away the greyhounds to their kennels. The great, arched room was dimly lighted by torches, suspended from rings in the walls, for it was the hour when the old lord, his two elbows resting on the arms of his chair, sank into the dreamland of the past.

Outside, according to the season, the green cornfields and heather appeared enchanted in the moonlight or the rambling of a storm over the crest of the hills was heard, and sometimes blinding flashes came with the rain, and the drops of water splashed against the great glass cupola.

Tonight, the old hall is besieged by November winds, groaning lamentably in every beam of the building, and the heavy doors, fastened with iron bolts, rattle noisily. Through the endless corridors of the fortress there are sounds which seem like the wailings of a soul in distress.

But though the wind might be angry, sweeping the snow or the dead October leaves about in the forest of the old domain, yet the moon beams softly on the roadway, making fantastic figures of the swaying wall flowers along the borders.

In winter or summer, spring or autumn, it is always the same sad hour for old Bertrand Du Guesclin, full of regrets, haunting memories and dreams of the past.

It is the hour for ghosts to come, followed by Sorrow, and, in her shadow, Fear. Always in this melancholy room Count Bertrand keeps his long vigil with Memory until late into the night Memory, sometimes appearing with her familiar face and silent footfall over the threshold of the low door. The old lord is lulled to sleep. His eyes grow dim, the lids close over them, and his arms drop down beside the chair. The names of former companions-at-arms, together on the battlefield, or stumbling about in pitiable drunkenness at banquets, sound in his ears. And in the weave of the tapestries he sees dream figures, in which he recognizes a gesture, or a smile, from the past, with still in their hands the flowers of youth, but with the gold and silk of their robes tarnished. The old man wakens, his long face is creased with wrinkles, and, clasping his old hands together, he heaves a deep sigh, as a tear rolls down his cheek.

Tiphaine!

Tiphaine! Above the visions of fire and blood; of red battlefields strewn with dead bodies under the mournful, cloudy sky; above the pleasures of triumphant marches headed with glistening banners of victory; above moonlight processions and ambuscades in the rain, comes the gentle, floating form of a young woman, a slender, graceful dame with beautiful white hands. Ah! the fair Tiphaine. She, whose smiles and caresses had cheered him and made his forty years seem young again, slowly appeared before him. As if a captive among the trees of this wonderful tapestry forest, she smiled at him across the branches of yellow apples, and around her head flew marvelous birds with brilliant colored plumage. Her clear, shining blue eyes seemed fixed upon him as she trod on the velvety turf and enchanted flowers.

Tiphaine!

He saw her again before him as she had appeared the first time, seated by a fountain near the edge of an old forest.

It was at dusk, a little before nightfall, and the shadows of the wood fell zigzag across the path. The last reflections of day made the trees seem golden in the fading light. The air was so heavy and sweet with the perfume of the forest that Du Guesclin was almost overcome by it, and while searching for some water he perceived her at the edge of a little fountain. Dressed in a long robe of cinder gray and a rose-colored mantle embroidered with wildflowers which clasped over the shoulders, she stood before him, motionless. White forms pressed about her, making a rustling noise with their wings, and the Count saw a flock of geese stretching out their long necks toward the unknown one.

How tall she seemed to him, almost a giantess; and, rude though it was, he stood still before this strange figure, looking so brilliant in the twilight as night advanced over the wild country.

He waited still, when suddenly the creature seated herself on a little stone bench and saluted him in a voice so sweet that he thought the drops of water were speaking.

"After tomorrow, Lord of Tombelaine," she said, "I will await you here, henceforth, every evening of my life, as I have done today."

Then all the geese arose from the ground with little cries. The dame appeared for a moment enveloped in a white shroud of wings, jewels seemed to sparkle in the tresses of her hair and from the border of her robe; then she was gone!

And every evening he returned, led there as if by some hand, to the edge of that fairyland where, if only to see the sunset behind this lovely dame, as the fading light fell upon her glittering gray and rose-colored gown, it gave his old heart joy.

For three months there were these tender meetings, three months of delicious pleasure, until the eve of Saint John, when, by the obscure light of the big forest, it was his privilege to go, accompanied with drums and flutes, to bring the beautiful bride to her marriage.

Oh, the return through the forest in the moonlight, the perfume of the hawthorn, and the velvety touch of the mosses under their feet! All the fairies of the wood were out that night in silk and satin, with torches and gold banners, to conduct the bride, in her white raiment, to the baronial domain of her betrothed.

And now across the tapestry he again sees the wedding ceremony, the deacons in their robes and the priest in his chasuble under a fringed canopy, the train of companions of the bride carrying in their little hands the tall stalks of lilies; then came beautiful maidens leading the dogs, and the soldiers, under their heavy armor, in honor of the fete. Next the children, laughing and happy, bearing between them bundles of lavender and the magic sprig-crystal.

The trailing robes of the ladies, the beautiful maidens, and the musicians made a fine procession through the forest in the moonlight.

Tiphaine!

He saw her again as mistress of the castle and saint in the chapel, surrounded by her women in her own apartment, embroidering on fine linen with gold thread, or attending to the flowers in the great black marble court of the castle. Here and there were pots of sunflowers, and she appeared like an angel among them, coming and going, accompanied by little pages who carried her purse, from which she gave abundantly to those who were in need. This was always the greatest joy of the rich and noble creature. He saw her pensive, charming face, with eyelids lowered and a smile upon her lips. Her cheeks were rose-colored, and her magic, golden tresses blew about her in the slightest breeze until she seemed to be invisible.

But oh, the fearful trickery of demons! She had deceived him! He gave ear to suspicions, and there was planted in his heart the poison of distrust, the poison which destroys love and uproots good faith.

Unhappy, indeed, had been the meeting! This unknown woman, at the hour of twilight, returned to her solitude and consecrated herself to evil gods, nymphs and genii.

This sudden love was followed by a malignant fever which came to him every night in the form of a dream, and he dreamed that, just as his name was pronounced in a voice like the dropping of water, the same flock of geese and phantoms evaporated in the darkness. All this held a charm over him, and, in spite of his efforts to shake it off, he remained a captive of his unfortunate love.

Paralyzed by fear, he had believed the suspicions, and bad reports against his gentle and devoted dame.

"In the night," they said, "she deserts your bed, calls her old companions, that you thought had been condemned, and, accompanied by a monstrous-headed goblin, she goes and gathers hemlock from the graves of dead lepers."

Full of horror and curiosity, he determined to follow and see if it were true. So one night he went to the threshold of the door which led out into the fields. But suddenly she turned and said to him:

"Never more, Lord of Tombelaine, shall I await you in the evening, as of yore, for the night of death has sounded for me: you have suspected Tiphaine; adieu."

Overcome with grief, he stood, clasping the little railing of the staircase. The beautiful creature became enveloped in the white moonlight, and, with a sound as of the fluttering of wings, she arose, and he never saw her more.

A PARTIAL LIST OF SNUGGLY BOOKS